The Famous
Adventures of
JACK

BERLIE DOHERTY

The Famous
Adventures of
JACK

Decorations by Sonja Lamut

GREENWILLOW BOOKS
An Imprint of HarperCollins*Publishers*

Library of Congress Cataloging-in-Publication Data
Doherty, Berlie.
The famous adventures of Jack / Berlie Doherty ; illustrated by Sonja Lamut.
p.   cm.
"Greenwillow Books."
Summary: In a magical land of giants and castles and beautiful princesses,
Jill hears several tales about characters named Jack, then embarks
on a fairy tale adventure of her own.
ISBN 0-06-623618-5 (trade).   ISBN 0-06-623619-3 (lib. bdg.)
1. Fairy tales—England. [1. Fairy tales. 2. Folklore—England.]
I. Lamut, Sonja, (date) ill.   II. Title.
PZ8.D6665 Fam   2001   [398.2]—dc21   00-067698

1 2 3 4 5 6 7 8 9 10   First American Edition

To the memory of
Katharine M. Briggs,
who saved hundreds of
folk stories from extinction

ONE DAY A GIRL WAS WALKING
through the forest and she came upon
an old woman sweeping leaves outside
the door of a cottage.

"Excuse me," the girl said. The old
woman stopped, and the leaves scuttled
like mice back to their heap outside her
door.

"Is this where Jack lives?" the girl
said.

"They're all called Jack around here,"
the old woman said. "Cousin Jack, Great-

grandfather Jack, Uncle Jack, son Jack, and some is daft and some is dead and some is disappeared. And some is lazy and good-for-nothing and waste-of-a-wishbone like my very own son. But they're all called Jack." She gave the leaves a last little stir with her broom. "You'd better come in."

Inside, the cottage was dark and very hot. Curled up in front of the flickering fire there was a black cat with a little white patch like a moon under his chin and another like a star on the tip of his tail. He yawned and stared at the girl, stretched himself full length, and then curled lazily back into a ball. The old woman flumped into a chair and slipped off her shoes. She put her feet on the cat and nodded at the girl.

"Which Jack did you want?" she asked. "They're ten a penny, Jacks are."

"I don't know," the girl said. "I met a man on the road who said it was high time I met Jack. He asked me to bring this to you because it would help me to find him." She held up a bag made of bits of this and bits of that: royal velvet and old sacking, satin and rags, knitted squares, and patches of flowered cotton.

"Did he now," the old woman replied. "And what was he like? Long, raggedy tangle of a beard, and a cloak that's got daylight coming through, I suppose. Eyes like a squirrel's hoard of nuts. Talks a load of nonsense. I know him all right."

"But as soon as he gave it to me, he disappeared."

"Let's see what he's sent me then, let's see." The old woman twitched her fingers impatiently, and the girl opened the bag and put her hand inside. She drew out a pouch made of old leather, fastened with a piece of frayed string, and the old woman leaned forward and snatched it from her. She pulled open the string and shook out the contents of the pouch onto her palm.

"Beans!" she said in disgust. "Well, we know what to do with them!" And quick as a girl she stood up, opened the latticed window behind her, and tipped the beans into the garden. The cat shuddered and licked her toes. "Anything else?"

The girl put her hand into the bag again and brought out a comb. "I like this," she said, putting it into her hair, where it shone as if it were studded with diamonds.

"What's that?" the old woman shrieked. "That's not a comb! Give it here!"

The girl pulled the comb out of her hair quickly and saw that the old woman was right; it wasn't a comb at all, but the skeleton of a fish. She threw it onto the old woman's lap, and for a moment it turned into a herring, gleaming and twisting, flashing with beautiful iridescent colors. The cat opened his green eyes and snapped his teeth together, but in an instant the fish turned back into a spine of bones, and the old woman trilled her fingernails along it and made it chime.

"The king of the herrings!" she laughed. "That's what this is! Would you like to hear about my great-grandfather Jack and the king of the herrings?"

"Yes, please," said the girl, who loved stories better than anything.

"Hmmph." The old woman cleared her throat and leaned back against her cushions. "Let's think then. . . ."

THE KING OF THE HERRINGS

Great-grandfather Jack's parents were very old and very poor when he was born. Not long after, his father died, leaving the boy in the care of an old, sick mother.

"I've done my best for you, son," she said when she, too, came to the end of her life. "You'll have to look after yourself now."

"I've had everything I could have wanted," Jack told her. "But I wish I'd known my father for longer."

Well, his mother died, and not long afterward, Jack was out working the square of bumpy land outside the cottage, and an old, gray-haired man came walking by. The old man paused, leaning on the rickety wall and looking at Jack, watching every move he made and nodding quietly and sadly to himself, till Jack asked him if there was anything he might like—a draft of water from the well, maybe, or a bite of bread and cheese.

"I was wondering," said the old man,

"if you might like to ride with me and seek your fortune."

Jack laughed and said, "I'll come with you gladly, but how can I ride when you don't have a horse?" and he put down his spade and came out of the gate. What should happen but the old man snorted into the air three times and turned into an old, shaggy gray horse. Jack scrambled onto his back, and off they went.

They had been riding along for a week and a day when they came to the sea, and there on the sand Jack found a herring, gasping for its life. Jack picked the fish up and tossed it back into the sea, and as it caught the light of the sun, it flashed like diamonds.

"That was the king of the herrings," said the horse. "You did well to give it back to the sea, Jack."

"I wouldn't have kept him. I wanted

him to live. But I'll have this feather."
And Jack jumped off the horse's back
again and picked up a silver-gray
feather that was fluttering on the
shoreline.

"Don't touch that," the horse said.
"It won't do you any good."

"I like it," said Jack, and he climbed
back onto the horse, put the feather in
his pocket, and forgot about it.

Not long after that they heard a
terrible moaning and groaning, and they
climbed away from the beach to see
what was happening. They found a
giant, lying in a ditch with his hands
clutching his head.

"I'm sick," groaned the giant. "I'm
dying. Help me, help me."

"Poor giant," said Jack. "I'm usually
scared of giants, but I'll see what I can
do."

He found a cloth to bind the giant's

head, and gave him food to eat, and helped him to stand up and stagger to his cave. There he built up a fire and made his bed neat for him so he could lie down in it and get well again.

"Thank you," rumbled the giant, and his voice echoed around the cave like thunder. "I won't forget what you did to help a giant."

"You did well," said the horse when Jack came back to him. "But I wish you hadn't picked up that feather."

"I'd forgotten about that." Jack brought the feather out of his pocket and looked at it. "No. I like it," he said, and put it back into his pocket.

Well, they traveled on, but they were getting tired and hungry by now, and they needed somewhere to rest. Through the trees they caught sight of a mansion, its windows glittering red in the sunset.

"That's a very fine place," said Jack. "I think I'll try my luck there."

The horse, for once, said nothing. They trotted up to the gates of the mansion, and when Jack offered his services to the master in exchange for food and rest, they were invited in.

The horse was put in the stables and given oats and straw and water, and nodded off among the fine black steeds of the master. Jack was given bread and stew in the kitchens and a bed of rushes to lie on if he wanted, though he chose to stay in the stables.

"I like it here," he said. "And I should like to serve the master."

But the maids in the kitchen only laughed at him and said, "What can you do for the master? Take your food and rest, and be on your way, that's the best thing for you."

His old horse said the same thing.

"Take your rest, and tomorrow we'll be on our way."

But during the night Jack had an idea. He remembered the feather in his pocket, and he took it out and sharpened it and made a pen out of it. Then he found some paper and some ink and wrote a letter to the master asking if he could be his servant. He wrote so carefully, and the writing on the page looked so beautiful, that the master sent for him at once.

"You write very well," said the master, stroking his pointy little beard. He couldn't take his eyes off the fancy curls and strokes of Jack's writing.

"Thank you," said Jack. "My mother taught me."

"Show me the pen that you wrote it with," said the master, and shaking a little with pride, and shaking a little with fear, Jack brought out the gray feather and laid it on the table. The master snatched it up at once, and in his hands it shone, for a moment, like silver. His eyes gleamed like greedy, bright fires.

"Bring me the bird that this came from," he ordered, "or you will lose your head."

Jack ran from the room and straight to the stables, where his old horse was standing waiting for him.

"What did I tell you about that feather?" the horse said gloomily. "Nothing but trouble, feathers."

"But please can you find the bird it came from?" Jack begged him.

"Oh, yes. I can do that. But it won't be the end of the story, believe me."

The horse took Jack down through the trees and back to the shore where they had found the feather. On a rock out at sea was a castle, shrouded in mist.

"That's where the bird lives," said the horse. "Whistle, and he'll come to you. Catch him quick, and take him to the master."

Jack stood on the shore and whistled, and out of the misty shape of the castle flew a great silvery gray bird, drifting across the sea toward them. When he'd caught the bird in his arms, Jack climbed onto the horse, and they rode through the trees, back to the mansion. Jack carried the bird to the master's room, and it was put into a cage, where it hung its head in silence.

"Poor bird, it's lonely now," said Jack.

"Lonely, is it?" The master laughed, rubbing his crackly hands together. "Bring me the princess who owns this bird, or you'll lose your head."

"I knew it," said the horse, who was waiting for Jack outside the stable.

"That feather spelled trouble to me as soon as I saw it."

"But can you take me to the princess who owns the bird?" Jack asked.

"I suppose so," said the horse, "but don't expect your troubles to be over."

They galloped back through the trees and onto the sand, and there was the castle, shrouded in mist across the green sea.

"She's in there," said the horse. "In the tower. You'll have to capture her if you're going to take her to the master."

"But how am I going to do that?" Jack asked.

With a sigh his horse stepped into the water, up to his fetlocks, up to his hocks, up to his withers, and then when it seemed he must drown, and Jack with him, he turned into a boat and floated right up to the castle. Jack scrambled out at once and clambered up the rocks to the castle, and there was the princess, looking down at him from the tower.

"You must come to my master," Jack told her.

"I will not," said the princess, who liked to speak her mind.

"Please come. If you don't, he's going to chop my head off."

Well, the princess's heart was as soft as butter really, so she agreed to come. "But that master of yours isn't going to come nosing around my castle, if that's what he's thinking," she said, and as soon as she was on the boat, she threw the keys of the castle over the side. They sank deep into the water, and the sea became as red as blood. A huge storm blew up, but somehow the creaking old boat reached shore, and when it touched the sand, it turned back into a horse, who shook himself so drops of water flew from his mane like diamonds. And then he carried Jack and the princess to the mansion.

The master rubbed his hands with glee when he saw the princess. He stroked her beautiful hair and looked into her deep dark eyes and sighed with love. Then he turned to Jack.

"Bring me her castle," he said. "Or I'll chop your head off."

The horse was waiting, still wet from his swim in the sea. "I'll do what I can, Jack," he said, "but you'll need more help than I can give you now."

He carried Jack to the giant's cave, and there they found the giant looking very fit and strong again.

"Will you help me?" Jack asked the giant. "My master wants the princess's castle, but how can I carry it to him?"

"Leave it to me," said the giant, and he waded across the sea and lifted up the castle on his shoulders as if it were a sack of potatoes and dumped it on the shore.

"No keys," he grunted, wiping his brow. "Your master ain't going to like that."

So Jack ran to the water's edge and cupped his hands around his mouth, calling into the waves, "King of the herrings, king of the herrings, please help me, or my master will have my head chopped off." Within seconds the fish leaped out of the sea with the keys of the castle dangling from his mouth. Jack took them, then climbed onto the horse's back.

"I'm in love with the princess," he said.

The horse snorted. "Don't think your troubles are over yet."

Jack put the keys in his pocket, and they followed the giant to the mansion. The giant put the castle down and shook hands with Jack, then shambled back to his cave.

Jack strode into the mansion and jangled the keys in the master's face. "You have your bird, you have your princess, you have your castle," he said. "Can I go?"

But the princess stepped between them and put her hand on Jack's arm. "You have a choice to make," she said. "One of you must be beheaded, yourself or the master. Which of you should it be?"

Jack looked at the princess with his mouth open; then he turned away and went to the window. He could see the king of the herrings leaping like diamonds in the sea. He could see the giant rolling down the green hills with flowers in his beard. Everything should be as free and happy as this, he thought.

"It's my fault, all this," he said. "If I hadn't picked up the feather, none of this would have happened. And now the bird is in a cage and you have to live with the master and your castle has been ripped from the sea. It's all my fault. I'm the one who should be beheaded."

"You have given the right answer," said the princess, and she kissed him. At once the guards ran in and dragged the master off to the dungeon to be beheaded.

The princess married Jack, and they lived in their castle in great happiness, and the old horse spent the last of his days eating hay and sweet grass, and watching Jack, and nodding happily to himself.

✤ There was a peaceful, satisfied sighing in the room when the old woman had finished telling her story. The girl looked around, surprised, and there seemed to be huddled shapes where there hadn't been shapes before, curled up on window seats and benches and the long, shabby sofa. The shapes seemed to move and turn and stretch, and then, strangely, didn't seem to be there anymore.

"What do you think?" the old woman said, stroking the cat with her bent old toes. "Did you like that story?"

"I loved it," the girl said. "It's the best story I've ever heard. But when you finished . . . I thought I heard . . . there seemed to be someone here . . ."

"Oh, everyone loves to listen to

stories. Especially when they're about themselves. What else have you got, Jill?"

"How did you know my name?" the girl asked, surprised.

"How do I know the stars shine? And I'm Mother Greenwood, in case you didn't know. Now then." She nodded at the bag, and Jill felt inside it and brought out a long leather belt. It had a heavy buckle shaped like a griffin's head, and carved into the leather there were strange words: *Hem yu an Kernow harth ha yonk neb a lathas an cawr Cormoran.*

Jill tried to read the words out loud, and instantly the cat leaped up, his hair standing on end and his back arched, and he circled the room, growling and snarling to himself, spitting.

But the old woman clapped her hands together. "Oh, my darling, I never thought I'd see that belt again!" she crooned, and her voice went as croaky and husky as a crow's. "Oh, the precious thing!" She took it from Jill and ran her fingers over the lettering, mumbling words that Jill couldn't understand.

"What does it say?" Jill asked, but Old Mother Greenwood shook her head and closed her eyes as if she was hugging great secrets to herself. "It's a language of long ago, that the Cornish folk used to speak. You won't be ready to read that yet."

"Does it belong to Jack? Is there a story about it?"

"Of course there's a story about it. There's a story about everything—but—"

The old woman shook her head. "It's not for you. Not at this time of night. Why, it would frighten the life out of you. Look at the cat, skimbled out of his wits. No, it's not for you, that tale."

She hung the belt on a hook by the fire, where it swung backward and forward like the pendulum of a clock. Tick, tick, tock, tock, and the griffin's head buckle gleamed like the sun itself. From his safe place on the top shelf of the dresser the cat watched it, his head swinging in time to its rhythm.

"Anything else in there?" said the old woman.

"It feels empty now," said Jill, disappointed. She felt in the bag again and pricked her finger on something sharp. It was a needle, black with age, but when she held it out to the old woman, it gleamed as if it was made of pure silver.

"Ha-ha!" Mother Greenwood rumbled with laughter. "Now I know this! This belongs to Daft Jack! He's one of the numskulls of the family, and no mistake. That's more like it! It'll just come in handy to darn this hole in my pinny, and while I'm doing it, I'll tell you all about him, the sorry nincompoop."

She tugged at her head and pulled out a long white hair, threaded the needle with it, and began to sew as she talked.

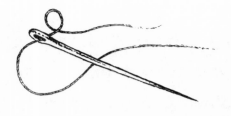

DAFT JACK

Daft Jack. Well, Daft Jack was sent to work one day by his mother. He didn't like work much, so she had to sweep him out of the house with a broom behind his heels. He helped a farmer to pull thistles out of his field, and for once in his life he worked so well that he earned a wage. And what the farmer gave him was this. This very needle. So Jack was very pleased, and he knew his mother would be, too. He stuck the needle in his hair and went home whistling, but he got a thirst on because the day was hot and he'd worked hard, so when he came to the river, he bent down and put his head in the water, and out slid the needle. It sank into the water like a little silver fish, and Daft Jack never even noticed.

Well, when he got home, his mother was pleased to know that he'd worked so well that the farmer had given him a wage. Oh, and a needle at that! Now she could sew patches on all the holes in his trousers.

She held out her hand for the needle, and Jack put his hand in his hair and felt about a bit and looked puzzled.

"It's gone, Mother," he said.

"Of course it's gone, you porridge-brain! Fancy putting a needle in your hair! Go back to work tomorrow, and this time put it in your pocket!"

Well, never in his life had Jack worked two days in a row, but he did as he was told, and the farmer was very pleased with him, and this time he paid him with a jug of milk. Jack remembered what his mother had said and put the jug in his pocket.

"Milk for supper!" he sang to

himself. "Won't Mother be pleased!"
He was so excited that he forgot about
being tired and ran all the way home.

"Milk! Good boy!" his mother said.
"Where is it then?" She held out her
hand, and he felt in his pocket and drew
out the jug. Empty! And wasn't his
trouser leg now beginning to feel very
damp where the cold milk had run down
the inside, and wasn't there a puddle of
milk on the floor where he was standing?

"It's gone, Mother," he said.

"Of course it's gone, you jelly-head!
Fancy carrying a jug of milk in your
pocket! Go back to work tomorrow, and
this time carry it back on your head.
And don't run!"

Work three days in a row! Well, Jack
did as he was told, and at the end of the
day the farmer gave him his wage. This
time it was a round of cream cheese.

"Cream cheese!" Jack sang, putting it

on his head as he'd been told. "How I do love a bite of bread and cream cheese. And Mother does, too."

And he strolled home, singing all the way, and the sun beat down on him and melted the cream cheese. By the time he got home it was running in sticky clots through his hair, down his forehead, around his ears, down his neck.

"Cream cheese today, Mother," Jack said, licking his lips.

"I can see that, you simpleton, you chump," said his mother, hitting him with her dishcloth. "Fancy carrying it on your head. Go back to work tomorrow, and bring it home safe in your hands."

Four days! Poor Jack trudged to work, and at the end of the day the farmer gave him his wage. This time it was a cat.

"A cat!" said Jack. "Why, it will kill all

the mice and rats that come nibbling around our door, and it'll keep me warm in bed at night. I'll carry you home safe in my hands like Mother said. Pussy pussy! Nice cat!" And he held out his arms and carried it away. But the cat hated being held. It scratched and bit and snarled and twisted, and in the end Jack dropped it, and away it ran, over the fields, and was never seen again.

"Well, where's your wage?" his mother demanded when Jack arrived home.

"It was a cat. But it's gone!" Jack said mournfully, holding out his scratched and bleeding hands for his mother to see, and hoping for a bit of comfort. But his mother wasn't in the mood for giving comfort, and she threw a bucket of cold water over him.

"Fancy carrying a cat in your hands!" she said. "You buttercup! You lazy daisy! Next time tie a bit of string around its neck."

So, it was the fifth day, and Jack was so tired that he crawled to work, and at the end of the day the farmer gave him his wage, and what should it be but a leg of mutton.

"My, oh, my!" Jack laughed, tying a piece of string around it. "Won't Mother be pleased!" And off he went, not running, and dragging the mutton behind him on its piece of string. "Mutton!" he called to his mother as he came to the house and she came running out.

"Where, Jack, where?" she asked, and he turned around to see that his leg of mutton had been chewed by dogs and covered in dust and dragged over stones until nothing was left of it but the bone.

"Gone!" he said.

His mother picked up the bone and

thwacked him with it, bish bash, over
his head.

"Blubber-brain!" she shouted.
"Mutton-face! Get back to the farmer
tomorrow, and this time, this time, carry
it over your shoulders!"

Six days! Jack hobbled to work,
hungry and tired, his hands sore from
scratches, his head sore from
thwackings, his scalp itchy with cream
cheese, but he worked all day, and the
farmer paid him. And this time the wage
was a donkey.

"A donkey!" said Jack. "I'll never have
to walk again! I can ride everywhere on
my donkey's back!" And he lifted the
donkey over his shoulders, as his
mother had told him, and set off for
home.

On his way home he passed the house
of a sad maiden, who couldn't speak,
and couldn't laugh, and who spent all

her days looking out of the window, feeling miserable. "The first person to make you laugh can marry you and live in riches for the rest of his life," her father said to her every day, but nothing ever happened to make her laugh.

But that day the girl heard a braying and a brawing and a heaving and a grunting, and she looked out of the window, and what should she see but Jack trudging along the lane with a donkey over his shoulders, and she burst out laughing.

"Look!" she called out, and her delighted father ran out of the house and into the street and invited Jack in at once to marry his daughter.

Which he did, of course, and he never had to work again, and his mother didn't have to put up with him any longer. And his wife laughed a lot, and they were all very, very happy.

✤ "Thank you," said Jill. "I'm glad he was happy in the end."

"Everybody's happy in the end," Mother Greenwood said. "That's the way of stories. Unless they're wicked, of course."

"Anyway," Jill said, "I haven't found the Jack I was looking for, and it's getting dark, so I suppose I'd better go."

"Oh, you can't go," the old woman chortled. "You haven't emptied that bag yet, have you?"

"So I haven't," said Jill, surprised. "I'm sure it was empty when I pricked my finger on that needle, but"—she groped inside the bag—"there's a box of some sort, and a ball, I think. And it feels like a grain of corn."

It had suddenly grown so dark that

she couldn't see anything anymore. The fire had died right down to a glow of ashes, and the old woman was snoring softly in her chair. All Jill could really see were the letters of the belt that hung by the fire, and they gleamed with a curious coppery green light of their own, words that made no sense to her. She stood up, meaning to touch it, but with a screech the cat leaped from the dresser onto her shoulders, digging his claws into her skin and making her jump with fright.

"Oh, all right, puss," she said. "All right. I won't touch it. I'd love to know why it's so important, though." She sank back into her chair and held the trembling cat in her arms. Gradually, as she stroked him, he began to purr, turning around and around on her knee as if he were trying to make a nest for himself, and it was such a comforting, rumbling sound that he made that she felt her eyes growing heavy and her eyelids beginning to droop. The cat was warm and heavy on her lap, and she felt herself nodding off to sleep, when what should creep into the silence but a voice, a purring and whiskery sort of voice, full of sleepiness and cream.

"Once upon a time," the voice said, and Jill knew that the old woman was fast asleep and snoring quietly, so it couldn't be her voice.

No, the voice was coming from the cat himself.

"Go on," she whispered.

"Once upon a time there was a king who had a beautiful daughter."

"They're always beautiful," sighed Jill.

"Do you want this story or not?" the cat asked, yawning. "It's meant to send you to sleep."

"Is it very long? I'm quite tired anyway."

"It's very long and very short," the cat said. "But at least it's not gruesome. It won't give you nightmares, like some of them." He shuddered and sank his claws ever so slightly into her leg and then closed them away again. "I don't like scary stories. Once upon a time, as I was saying, there was a king who had a beautiful daughter, and all the princes wanted to marry her. But the king said that he would only give her away to the one who could tell a story that never ended. And the ones who couldn't tell an endless story would have their heads chopped off for wasting his time," he said quickly, "only I don't like that bit much. Anyway, Jack, nephew of that other Jack, was out walking one day, and he thought, I might as well have a go at this, so he knocked at the door of the castle and told the king that he had a story for him. 'Go on then,' said the king, and he nodded to his executioner to sharpen his blade, but I hate that bit, too. So Jack began his story, and it went like this. . . .

"There was a man who built a barn that was so high that it reached up to the sky, and was so wide that it reached from east to west till it got to the end, and so long that it reached from north to south till it got to the end, and he filled it full as full from top to bottom and side to side with grains of corn. And there was a little hole in the roof. And one day a little jenny wren hopped through the hole, but she could only fit one grain of corn into her beak, and she flew out again with it. And another day another jenny wren hopped in and took one grain of corn and flew away with it. And another day another jenny wren came in and took one grain of corn and flew away . . . and another day another jenny wren hopped in and—"

But Jill had stopped listening, because the room had grown very cold, as if the door had been opened. There was a sound as if somebody was creeping very softly across the floor. A dark shape was shadowed across the glowing heart of the fire as if someone was standing in front of it.

"And another day another jenny wren hopped in and took a grain of corn, and another day another—"

And the belt with the gleaming letters and the griffin's head buckle was traveling across the darkness, as if someone had lifted it off its hook and was carrying it across the room. *Hush, hush* went the feet on the floor, and Jill's heart stood still with listening.

"Another jenny wren came in and took a grain of corn and flew away, and then another day—"

There was a sigh as if the door had closed, and the gleam of the letters disappeared, and the breath of cold air had gone.

"Took another grain of corn," the cat went on, and Jill yawned a long, deep yawn—"and flew away, and another day"—the cat's voice began to fade and stretch as he yawned and yawned again—"another jenny wren . . . in the end the king couldn't stand it any longer, and said he was dying of boredom because the tale was never going to end, and told Jack to stop at once and marry his daughter, please."

But Jill never heard the end of the story because she was fast asleep.

When Jill woke up the next morning, the cat had gone, and the sun was pouring through the window. There was a cauldron of porridge hanging on a hook over the fire, and on a little stool in front of Jill there was a bowl and spoon and a pot of honey and a blue jug brimming with creamy milk.

"So, you're awake, are you?" Mother Greenwood said. "Run outside and splash some water on your face, and then your breakfast will be ready. We'll have to set off soon. There's been a thief in the night." She jerked her head toward the hook that the belt had hung from. "And if we don't find that belt, there'll be trouble, believe you me. Go on. Be quick."

Jill went outside. In the middle of the garden there was a well, and she wound down the bucket until she could feel that it had dipped into the water, and pulled it up again. Out of the bucket jumped the cat, soaked to the skin and his fur bedraggled and ratty, and shivering with fright and anger. He snarled at Jill and ran into the house, and Jill looked into the water in the bucket and saw, briefly, a face that was not her own, a huge, ugly bearded face. She looked away, too frightened to think, and when she looked back, there was her own face. She put in her hands and cupped up some water and splashed herself. It was so cold that she gasped out loud.

I must have been half asleep, she thought, and that could have been true because when she went back into the house, there was the cat curled up in her chair, fast asleep and completely dry.

"Eat up," Old Mother Greenwood said. "There's no time to lose."

She scurried around the room while Jill was eating, gathering together a few pieces of bread and cheese, which she tied up in a red spotted handkerchief and put into a basket. Jill ate as fast as she could, which was difficult because the porridge was hot and pretty lumpy. She was distracted by a scratching sound coming from outside the window, and when she looked up, she could see the nodding head of the top of a plant just outside. She finished her porridge and put the bowl down, and when she looked up again, the plant seemed to have grown a little higher. It was very strange. She went to the window to look at it, but the old woman called to her sharply from the doorway.

"Come on," she said. "There's no time for looking at beanstalks. We've got to go."

Jill picked up her bag and hurried

after her. "But where are we going, Mother Greenwood, and why are we in such a hurry?"

"If we don't get that belt back, Lord knows what will happen to all of us. Come on."

She ran ahead, and it was all Jill could do to keep up with her. The cat scampered after them, yowling at them to wait for him.

"Where are we going, though?" Jill panted.

"Cornwall, looks like."

"Is it far?"

The old woman tutted impatiently. "It's near and it's far. It depends where you're starting from, doesn't it? A better question to ask would be, How long will it take us to get there? And the answer to that is, A long time if you can't walk faster than that."

"I'm doing my best," said Jill. "How long will it take if I walk as fast as you?"

"Do we have to have all these questions?" growled the cat, jumping up onto the old woman's shoulder and curling himself like a scarf around her neck. "There's only one way to make a long journey short anyway."

"What's that?" Jill asked, and the old woman stopped running and wagged her head at her.

"Fancy not knowing that! The way to make a long journey short is by telling a story to pass the time away."

"I know a good story. There was a man who built a barn that was so high," the cat began, "that it reached up to the sky, and was so wide that it reached from east to west till it got to the end, and so long that—"

"I've heard that one," said Jill. She felt inside her bag and brought out the ball. "There must be a story about this."

"Throw it to me," Mother Greenwood said. She caught it smartly with one hand and tossed it back to Jill. But when Jill caught it, it had turned into an apple.

"Oh, an apple! How lovely!" she said, and was just about to bite into it when the old woman clapped her hands and the apple flew out of Jill's grasp and into hers.

"You mustn't eat this." She chuckled. "It belongs to the magic castle!" She flung the apple high into the air, and when it landed, it burst open and the pieces scattered for miles, and wherever they fell, they turned into flowers. The pips all landed together and became a wrought-iron gate, very curled, very spiky, and very high, and a wall grew from each side of them and closed in the flowers. Jill ran to the gate and peered in. She could see a beautiful garden, with a lake that was as blue as the sky. Three swans floated there, two white ones and a black one. And beyond the lake, so far away it could only just be seen, a castle.

"Is that the magic castle? Does a king live there?" she asked.

"He did once," the old woman said, "and that's the beginning of the story. And now someone else lives there, and that's the end of the story. Want to know the middle?"

"Yes, please," Jill said.

"Climb on then."

Jill turned around and saw that the cat had grown to the size of a horse and was pawing the ground impatiently, and that the basket Mother Greenwood had been carrying over her arm had become a carriage that was hitched up behind him. She climbed up next to Mother Greenwood, and the cat trotted neatly along the track that led to Cornwall. And Jill sat back and listened to the story of the magic castle.

THE MAGIC CASTLE
AND THE APPLES
OF IMMORTALITY

In the orchard of the magic castle was a
tree that grew the apples of immortality.
It was guarded by giants and dragons,
and the king who lived there had a
beautiful daughter. He loved her so
much that he never wanted her to leave
him, so he had put her under a spell.
That's the beginning of the story.

Now, there was also, far away from
there, a lord who had three sons, and
the youngest of them was my great-
grandfather's uncle Jack. Well, the lord
was dying, and he told his sons that the
only way they could save him was by
bringing him the apples of immortality.
The older two brothers didn't even
bother to go and search for them
because they knew that when their

father died, they would have all his money. So they hid. But Jack was a kind lad who loved his father. He'd do anything to save him, and he wandered for miles and miles until he came to a lonely cottage. Inside was an old, old man who could hardly walk and could hardly talk, but he listened to Jack's story and said yes, he could help him find the apples of immortality.

"Come in and rest," he whispered in his tiny, wispy voice, "and tomorrow I'll give you a good black horse to ride."

He shuffled across the room and pulled back a curtain to show Jack where he must sleep. "Lie down. Vipers and worms will wriggle all over you tonight, but you must ignore them or you'll turn into one yourself. Good night." And he blew out the candle and shuffled away.

Well, it was just as he said, and poor

Jack had a terrible night trying to lie still while snakes and worms slithered all over his face. Can you imagine that!

But next morning there was a fine black horse waiting for him outside the cottage. The old man gave Jack a ball of black wool and told him to hold one end of it and to fling the ball of wool as far as he could between the horse's ears and follow it. So Jack did, and the wool led him to another cottage, where another old man, even older and frailer than the first one, shuffled to the door and said he could help him to find the apples.

"I'll show you where you can sleep tonight," he croaked, leading Jack to the curtained shelf by the fire, "but you must lie very still when the spiders and the stinging ants crawl over you, or you'll turn into one yourself. And tomorrow there'll be a fine gray horse waiting to take you on your way."

And it was just as he said. Ants crawled all over Jack's face, and spiders wriggled through his hair, but he lay as still as he could.

Next morning there was a gray horse waiting for him, and the old man gave him a ball of silver thread and told him to fling it between the horse's ears as far as he could and follow the trail.

Jack followed it until he came to another cottage at the side of a blue lake. There an old, old man was sitting outside the cottage in a rocking chair, whittling a reed into a pipe.

"You've come to find the castle of the golden apples, and you're very near, and you're very far," he breathed, so faint that Jack had to put his head right up to him to hear him. "I'll let you sleep well tonight, Jack, to prepare yourself. Come inside."

Next day he brought Jack down to the shore of the lake.

"Can you see the castle, Jack?" he asked, and Jack could just make it out, far away and held in the water's reflection like a still, shimmering fish.

"For one hour the castle will be under a spell," the old man said. "Everyone in it will be asleep. Run in quickly, and take the apples from the orchard. But remember this: If you stop more than once, you will be caught in the spell yourself and will never escape."

Then he drew out his reed pipe and played such a sweet tune on it, and three swans came sailing across the lake to him.

"Come swans white,
   come swan black,
Come swans three and
   ferry young Jack
Over the deeps of the
   crystal lake."

So Jack stood with one foot on each
of the white swans, and the black swan
lifted her wings for him to steady
himself, and they sailed across the lake
to the enchanted castle.

Four giants lay snoring at the gate,
and Jack tiptoed past them. Four
dragons slept at the great doorway, and
their breath was fire that scorched the
earth around them. Jack tiptoed past
them. All around him servants lay
sleeping. He crept through the kitchens,
where the maids and cooks lay with
their heads on the tables, and out he ran

into the orchard. He picked up three golden apples from the grass, quick, quick.

But he'd never been inside a castle before, and he ached to see the great hall. He opened the door and peeped in. There was the king, fast asleep on his throne. There was the queen, a mirror raised in her hand and her eyes tight shut. There were the slumbering courtiers, folded up on the floor like neat bundles of clothes. He crept past them all, and up the stairs, and came to a room at the very top. There on a couch lay the princess of the castle, deep in her enchanted sleep, and she was so beautiful that Jack knelt down and kissed her. How he longed to stay with her, because he'd fallen in love, you see. But he daren't. He took the ring from his finger and slipped it onto

hers as a sign that he loved her. Then
he ran as fast as he could down the
stairs, past the dragons, past the giants,
to where the swans were waiting for
him.

> "Come swans white,
>   come swan black,
> Come swans three and
>   carry me back
> Over the deeps of the
>   crystal lake."

In his hurry he dropped one of the
apples, and at that instant the
enchantment stopped. The giants
roared, but they were too late. The
dragons snarled, but they were too
late. Jack was away on the backs
of the swans before they could
reach him.

❖ Old Mother Greenwood clicked her tongue, and the cat lowered his head and stood still.

"And did Jack ever see the princess again?" Jill asked.

"Oh, there's a lot more to the story yet," said Old Mother Greenwood. "I'm just stopping to check our route."

She held up a ring that was shaped like a griffin's head and turned it this way and that until it sparkled in the light of the sun, as red as rubies.

"Halfway there," she said. "Time to eat." She opened up the red scarf and shared out half the bread and cheese among the three of them and put the rest in Jill's bag.

"I'd rather have mouse," grumbled the cat.

"You'd need a mouse as big as a cat to feed you now," Mother Greenwood said. "And I don't know where you'll find one of those. So you'd better eat cheese or do without."

Jill ate her food dreamily, as if there were a spell about her. She was still caught in the story about the apples of immortality, imagining the swans on the blue lake, and the beautiful sleeping princess, and the golden apples. Old Mother Greenwood nodded off to sleep for a bit, and the cat curled himself up and purred, loud and rumbling as a horse. When they woke up, they drank from a stream, and then they set off again.

"Well, the old man was waiting for Jack by the shore," went on Mother Greenwood.

He seemed to have aged another hundred years. His toenails and fingernails were long and gnarled and twisted, and his skin was dropping away from him like bark peeling off a tree. Jack showed him the apples and said he must hurry to his father with them straightaway. "But I must give you a reward for helping me," he said.

"There's only one thing I want," the old man said. "I'd like you to chop off my head, please." And he knelt down by a well.

"It's not much of a reward," said Jack.

"Please do it, though."

So Jack did as he was told, and as soon as the head dropped into the well, a young acrobat jumped up in the old man's place and began doing cartwheels and handstands across the grass.

"Mystery, mastery, my magic is back!" he sang happily. "Tell my brother!"

Jack rode back the way he had come and met the second old man, who asked him to do the same thing, and he turned into a jester, tossing ten colored balls at a time into the air and catching them behind his back.

"Ants and spiders, my magic is back!" he shouted. "Tell my brother!"

Jack rode on and came to the third old man, and when his head was chopped off, he turned into a conjurer, who drew white doves out of his pockets and blew butterflies out of his mouth.

"Snakes and worms! My magic is back!" He laughed. "Thank you, Jack."

Well, Jack had to get back to his father, didn't he? He rode on his way with his apples in his pockets, and just before he reached his father's house, he met his brothers, idle as usual and floppy with drink.

"I found the apples," he called to them, as pleased and excited as a puppy. "Look!" And he showed them the delicious-looking apples.

The brothers looked at each other and scowled. Ah, they could see what would happen now, all right. Their father would be cured, and Jack would certainly become his favorite son. Do you think they were pleased about this? Without having to say anything to each other, they each thought of the same plan.

"Sleep first," the oldest one told Jack.

"It wouldn't do for Father to see you looking so tired," the other one said.

And while Jack was asleep, they stole the apples. They replaced them with two poisoned ones, and then they hurried to their sick father's bedside and gave him the apples of immortality.

Well, when Jack arrived at his house the next morning, he was very surprised to see his father up and well again.

"See what your wonderful brothers have done for me!" The lord laughed. "I'm cured!"

"But I've brought you the apples of immortality, Father," Jack said, and produced the two apples that his brothers had hidden in his pockets.

"Those are poisoned!" the oldest brother said at once. "Jack's trying to poison you, Father!" And it seemed to be true: One sniff of the apples was enough to turn the old lord's stomach sour.

"Behead him, behead him!" the brothers demanded. Well, the lord was beside himself with grief, but he agreed that Jack must be beheaded. He asked the executioner to take Jack out to the woods and behead him there, because it would break his heart to let it happen near home.

Now, the executioner had known Jack since he was a little lad, and there was no way he was going to chop off his head. So, as soon as they reached the woods, he told Jack he could go free. And no sooner had he said that than a big gray bear appeared, picked Jack up, and ran off with him, which made Jack think that his time had come after all. But after a while the bear set Jack down again and lifted off his own head. Who should it be but the conjuring magician. "You can live with us," he told Jack. "You're quite safe now." So Jack lived in exile with the magic brothers and was nearly happy. But not completely. He had kept his head, but he had lost his heart, hadn't he?

And what about the princess? When she woke up, she remembered the kiss straightaway, and she knew it hadn't been a dream. And wasn't there a fine, sparkling ring on her finger that hadn't been there before? So she told her father, the king of the castle, that she had fallen in love and that she must find her young man or she'd never be happy, and at last he released her from her spell and let her go. So she came over the blue crystal lake and went in search of the owner of the ring. But it seemed hopeless. It's a big world.

Anyway, after a long time her search brought her to the mansion where the lord and the two older brothers lived.

"Was it you who kissed me?" she asked the first brother. She was very beautiful, so he said yes. She took off the ring and tried to put it on his finger, but it was so tight that it stuck before it reached the first knuckle, and his finger swelled up like a balloon around it, and it took all of his father's servants, wrenching and twisting, to get it off again.

The princess asked the second son, "Was it you who kissed me?" and she was so beautiful that he said yes. She tried to slip the ring on his finger, but it grew sharp teeth on the inside and bit into his flesh till he bled.

"Have you no more sons?" she asked the lord, and his eyes filled up with tears. He said his third son was dead, and he was sorry with all his heart.

At that moment there was a flurry of trumpets, and in tumbled an acrobat, a juggler, and a conjurer, in a whirlabout of music and color and jiggery dancing and sparkling lights, and behind them ran Jack. He stopped still and stared at the princess, and he knew her at once. And when he kissed her, she knew him. She put the ring on his finger, and of course it fitted perfectly.

"Will you marry me, Jack?" she said.
And he said, "Yes."

So they went back to the magic castle, and there they lived and there they live and there they will live till the end of their days.

And that's the end of the story, and here we are in Cornwall.

✛ "It was a lovely story," said Jill. "The best story I've ever heard. I hope the two brothers had their heads chopped off."

"Don't!" The cat shuddered. "How can you be so gruesome!"

"It's only a story." Jill laughed.

"*Only* a story," the cat repeated, astonished. "How can you say that? What's *only* about a story?"

"Well, I mean, it isn't real," said Jill, trying to think about that. "There's no such things as magic castles and giants and things. But anyway, it got us here in no time, like you said."

"So can I stop being a horse now?" And before he'd finished saying it, the cat had shrunk right down to his normal size. He ran up a tree and down again, pounced at a passing butterfly, and set to licking himself thoroughly. No horse could do this, he thought, lifting his back leg behind his ear.

The carriage had become a basket again, upside down on the grass, and Mother Greenwood and Jill had both tumbled out with their legs in the air.

Old Mother Greenwood dusted herself down and walked to the end of the sand track, where it disappeared into a milky green sea.

"How I do love the sound of the sea!" She sighed. "It makes me think of the wind about my trees. Now, Jill, do you see that little island hiding in the mist across the water?"

"I think I do," Jill said.

"That's called St. Michael's Mount. And do you see the turrets of a castle?"

"Just about."

"That's the giant's castle. That's where you'll have to go to get the belt back."

"Me?"

"You and the cat."

The cat stopped washing himself and hurtled back up the tree, every hair of his body standing on end. "No, no, no," he howled from the very top branch. "I won't and I won't and I won't. I'd rather be a horse again. I'd rather eat bread for the rest of my life. No, no, no, don't make me go to the giant's castle."

"Or me," said Jill. "I couldn't possibly."

"But you have to," said Old Mother Greenwood. "I'm much too old to go. Besides, didn't you both watch the belt leave the cottage last night?"

"Yes," Jill confessed. "But I was listening to a story at the time."

"And I was *telling* the story," said the cat from up the tree, "a very interesting story. I could tell it again if you like. . . . There was a man"—he jumped down, landing neatly at Jill's feet and gazing up at her with earnest green eyes— "who had a barn . . ."

"All right, I'll go to the island," said

Jill quickly. "But not on my own. The cat will have to come, too."

"I can't swim," the cat purred. He rubbed himself around her ankles prettily. "Sorry. I couldn't possibly go." He stepped into the basket and curled himself into a comfortable ball.

"That reminds me of something that happened this morning," Jill said slowly, staring at the basket. "I was getting water from the well . . . I wound up the bucket . . . and the cat was in it."

"It wasn't me," mumbled the cat. "I never go near water."

"If this was a bucket, instead of a basket," said Jill, "the cat could sail across to the island in it." And before she'd finished speaking, the basket had turned into a bucket at her feet, and the startled cat was trying to scramble out.

"Clever girl," said Mother Greenwood. She picked up the bucket, stuffed the cat back down inside it, and pushed him out to sea.

"But you don't understand." The cat's head appeared briefly again over the rim of the bobbing bucket and then disappeared as he ducked back down. "It isn't just water I'm afraid of," he wailed in a tinny, buckety, echoey voice. "It's giants. I'm terribly frightened of giants."

"Look after Jill." Old Mother Greenwood chuckled, and she gave Jill a little nudge that sent her tumbling head over heels into the sea. "Good-bye!"

It was nearly dark when they arrived at the island. The sun was setting lemony and watery behind the horizon, and a gibbous moon was rising. Jill scrambled onto the gritty sand and lodged the cat's bucket in a hollow between two rocks. They both gazed up at the gray walls of the castle. The birds of the sea wailed from its turrets, high above their heads.

"Oh, no," said the cat. "I'm not going in there."

"We have to," said Jill. "You heard what Mother Greenwood said. Anyway, I'm sure there aren't any giants left in this country. They belong to long ago."

"But sometimes it *is* long ago."

"Come on." Jill picked the cat up and

walked steadily toward the castle. Her heart fluttered inside her like a bird trying to beat free, and she could feel the cat's chest thumping wildly against her hand. He put a soft paw each side of her neck and buried his face in her hair. They came to the great door of the castle, which was studded with iron bolts and had a knocker shaped like a griffin's head, flaking with yellow rust. Jill put the cat down and pushed open the door.

Silence. A deep and dark and utterly dreamy silence. They tiptoed in. Dusty banners hung from the walls, with threads of spiderwebs hanging from them. Bats fluttered soundlessly around Jill's head. Jill edged her way forward through the great dusty hall and into another room. She looked back to see if the cat was following her. All she could see of him was the white moon under his chin and the little white star at the end of his tail. He padded bravely toward her and then suddenly froze, arched his back, and leaped back into her arms.

Now she could hear what he could hear. In another room someone was snoring, deep and steady and slow: in, out, in, out, like waves crashing onto the shore, in, out, in, out.

For a long time Jill and the cat stood still, listening to the snoring, trying to work out where it was coming from. As her eyes grew used to the swimmy darkness, Jill could just make out a flight of stone steps leading up to another floor. So the giant was up there, in his bed, and, by the sound of it, fast asleep.

Step by soundless step Jill and the cat climbed the stairs, one step to each rumbling snore. It seemed to take forever. They came to a long passage. At the end of it was a room lit by a flickering candle. The door was not quite shut. Jill squeezed the cat, ever so slightly, to let him know that she was going to go inside. She could feel his whiskers, tight as wires, against her cheek.

And slow as dreamers they stepped into the giant's room. The candle was on the floor, and though they couldn't make out the giant, they could see his huge, slumbering shadow thrown up against the wall. And curled around the candleholder, like the cast-off skin of a snake, was the belt, with its griffin's head buckle and its green lettering gleaming like tiny, watching eyes.

Then Jill did the bravest thing she had ever done in her life. She stepped forward, one step, two steps, three, without a breath escaping from her lips, four steps, five, six, till the belt was at her feet. Then she bent down, slowly, slowly, and slid her fingers around it.

At that moment the snoring stopped. The sleeping giant sat up and reached out for the candle. Jill screamed and dropped the belt. And that was when the cat did the bravest thing *he* had ever done. He leaped out of Jill's arms and flung himself in the direction of the giant's face. He was a flying bundle of spit and claw and scratch and bite, a snarling, yowling rocket of fight, and the giant flung his arms up and yelled with fright and pain and ran for the door. But Jill was running, too, with the belt in her hand, and she and the giant collided into each other. They both stopped, trembling.

"You're not a giant," said the giant, in a very small, young voice. He bent down and picked up the candle and held it up, and now Jill could see that *he* wasn't a giant either, but a boy, not much older than herself.

"That's not a giant. It's Jack!" said the cat in disgust.

"Cat!" said the boy. "It's you!" He bent down and picked up the cat and made a great fuss of him, and the cat made a great fuss of Jack, nuzzling into his neck and purring down his ear, wrapping himself into his arms, rasping his rough pink tongue along his fingers.

While this was going on, Jill put the belt into her bag for safekeeping. She held up the candle to look around the room and saw that there was a fireplace laid with wood for a fire, so she dipped the candle into it and instantly had a good blaze going. She took the bread and cheese out of the red spotted handkerchief and put them on the hearth.

"You've got blood all over your face," she told Jack. "Sit down, and I'll try and mop you up. And you'd better tell me why you stole this belt from Mother Greenwood's cottage. I've got to take it straight back to her as soon as it's daylight, or something awful will happen."

The cat spread himself full length in front of the fire just as if this were his home and he were master of it.

Jack knelt down next to Jill, and she dabbed at his cheek with the handkerchief.

"Ouch," he said.

"Stop squirming. I'm being as gentle as I can. And as you're a thief, you should be grateful that I'm trying to help you at all. Have some bread and cheese to take your mind off the pain."

"He's not a thief. He's Jack Greenwood," mumbled the cat, half asleep
with one green eye open. "My best
friend. And I nearly killed him!" He
chuckled in a purry way and licked
Jack's hand again with his gritty
tongue.

"So you're Mother Greenwood's lazy,
good-for-nothing, waste-of-a-wishbone
son!" Jill said. "I've heard about you."

"Have you? So she's still grouchy
with me, is she?" Jack asked. He rubbed
his nose glumly. "I was sent to her in
her old age because she made a wish on
a chicken bone, but she seems to think it
was a bad mistake. She'd always wanted
a baby, and she got me! I've been an
awful disappointment to her. I had to
leave home in the end because I sold

our cow for a bag of beans. She sent me away to find the man who'd given them to me, but I couldn't find him again, so I just left the beans by the roadside."

"Were they in a little brown pouch?" Jill asked. "Well, that's funny. A man in a tattered old cloak gave them to me."

"That was him!" said Jack.

Jill laughed. "And I gave them back to Mother Greenwood. No wonder she chucked them out of the window! But it wasn't the only thing he gave me. He gave me lots of things to take to her, including that belt." She took it out of her bag again and held it up to the fire-light. "Your mother was really happy when she saw that."

"Anyway," Jack went on, "as I was

saying, I couldn't get Blossom back, so I didn't dare go back home. But one night I looked in through the window, and I saw that belt by the fire, and I thought, That's the famous Cornish belt, that is, that Mother told me about. I'll take that back to Cornwall and see if I can seek my fortune. Then Mother will be pleased with me, surely. So I sneaked in and stole it. But when I got here, nobody would touch it. They said it was far too dangerous. Someone told me to take it across to the giant's castle. I was very frightened, I can tell you. And when I got here, I was scared to go back again in the dark. I must have fallen asleep, and then I woke up and I thought the giant was in the room, and then he attacked me and tried to rip my face off, and it was you, Cat! It was you all the time!"

He fussed and tickled the cat all over again, and the cat screwed himself up into a helpless, giggling bundle. "Anyway, it's much better now you're here, too, and the fire's lit and there's food to eat. I quite like it here. And I'm not scared now."

"We must leave as soon as it's light," said Jill. "And we musn't go to sleep, Jack. We must listen out in case the giant comes. If there is one. I don't think I believe in giants . . . but . . . well, things are getting very strange. We must stay awake. We could do with a story to pass the time away."

"I know one," muttered the cat, and Jack tickled him again.

"I wish you'd tell me the story about that belt," Jill said.

"I only know it's to do with a very famous Jack," said Jack. "And it comes from Cornwall."

"And it's very gruesome," the cat mumbled.

"Do you know anything about this rusty box? It's the last thing in the bag."

Jill pulled out the little rusty box and showed it to Jack. He turned it over and rubbed it on his sleeve, and it began to gleam as if it was made of pure gold. He lifted the lid, and it was full of a black, powdery mixture. He took a pinch of it in his fingers and sniffed at it and immediately sneezed so violently that the cat's bones nearly jumped out of his skin and the fire flattened down like a frightened hen.

"Id's snuff!" sniffed Jack. His eyes were streaming. "This snuffbox belonged to Great-grand-uncle Jack, who was the luckiest man in the world. Jack and the golden snuffbox." He blew his nose on the spotted handkerchief. "Oh, yes, I know this story."

"Lovely!" said Jill happily. She poked the fire to make the flames dance again. "Go on then."

JACK AND THE GOLDEN SNUFFBOX

Well. My great-grand-uncle Jack lived in the forest with his mother and father. It was very quiet in the forest, and lonely, with only the great dark trees and the birds who lived in them for company, and Jack had a hankering to know what the rest of the world was like. So one day he told his mother that he was leaving home to go traveling.

"Go if you must," said his mother, "and I'll bake you a cake to take with you. Would you like a small cake with my blessing or a large cake with my curse?"

"A large cake," said Jack.

When it was ready, he wrapped it up and went away with it, and his mother stood at the doorway of the cottage, cursing him until he was out of sight.

Jack met his father and told him he

was going traveling and that he had a large cake with his mother's curse in it to take with him.

"Then take this as well," his father said, and gave him a golden snuffbox, which he must only use to save his life. And with these things, Jack left his home in the forest forever.

When he finished the cake, he had to find someone to give him his next meal, and he knocked at the door of a mansion house. A girl let him in.

✛ "And was she beautiful?" Jill interrupted.

The cat sighed. "Of course she was. It's a story, isn't it? Go on, ignore her."

So Jack went on.

A beautiful girl let him in, and she sent for her father, who asked Jack what he could do in exchange for his keep.

"I can do anything," the Jack in the story boasted, and the beautiful girl smiled at him. His heart fluttered like a butterfly, and he could hardly take his eyes off her as she went past him to her room.

"The insolent youth has fallen in love with your daughter," the lord's chief servant whispered. "Chop his head off!"

The lord was amused, because he knew his servant was a jealous type. "If the boy wants to marry my daughter," he said, "he must put a lake in front of my house by eight in the morning, with large men-of-war sailing on it. They must fire a royal salute in my honor, and the last round must fly in through the window and break the leg of my daughter's bed. Can you do that?"

"Yes, sir," said Jack.

"Good," said the lord. "Because if you don't, you can say good-bye to this world."

"Yes, sir," said Jack. He was feeling a bit fluttery by now, but as soon as the lord had gone, he took the snuffbox out of his pocket and opened it up, and out jumped three little men, as nifty as soldier boys, and they asked Jack what he wanted.

"You go to sleep," they told him, "and we'll get it done."

And so they did. Next morning the servant was furious, but the lord of the house was so pleased with the lake and the men-of-war sailing on it and the firing of the royal salute that broke his daughter's bed, that he asked if Jack could do anything else for him.

The daughter touched Jack's hand, and he gulped and said, "Yes, sir. What would you like?"

"What I want is this," said the lord, clicking his tongue as he thought. "Let me see. Ah, yes! A castle on twelve golden pillars, with a hundred soldiers drilling in the yard in front of it. That'll do."

The pleased servant smiled behind his hand.

"If you manage it, you can marry my daughter," the lord went on. "But if you don't . . ." And he drew his finger across Jack's throat. "See?"

"Yes, sir," said Jack, and as soon as the lord was gone, he opened up the snuffbox and asked the little men to help him, and by eight o'clock it was done. There on the hill overlooking the mansion was the mightiest castle anyone had ever seen, standing proud and magnificent on twelve golden pillars, and a hundred smart soldiers parading in its courtyard.

The servant nearly passed out with shock when he saw it, but the lord was very impressed.

"Wonderful," he said. "I don't know how you do it. I suppose you think you've won my daughter now?"

"Yes, sir." Jack's heart started pounding. He smiled at the daughter and she smiled back, as rich as a blossoming rose with happiness, but her father shook his head and sent her out of the room.

"Can't have her yet. I need all the trees felled around the mansion. By eight o'clock, Jack. You know what will happen if you do it. And you know what will happen if you don't."

"Yes, sir," said Jack, and no sooner was the lord's back turned than he opened up his snuffbox and gave his orders to the little men, and they had the whole area cleared of trees by eight o'clock sharp, with not a twig or a leaf left.

The servant was so furious that he stamped around the clearing till the soles of his boots fell off.

"I can't help but admire you," the lord said to Jack. "And I'm a man of honor. You may marry my daughter today."

Jack was the happiest young man in the world. He smiled and smiled till his cheeks were round as apples, and his beautiful bride danced in his arms and told him she would love him till the day she died.

"And we'll have lots of children," they promised each other.

"And they'll all be as clever as you," she promised him.

"And they'll all be as beautiful as you," he promised her.

The wedding feast lasted three days,

and ended with a midnight ball outside on the lawns of the castle. You could hear the music for miles and miles. But the chief servant had no heart for dancing. He decided to find out how Jack did all these magic things.

So while everybody else was out having fun, he crept into the golden castle and ferreted through Jack's belongings, which were very few, and there he found the golden snuffbox, snug in Jack's pocket. Of course he opened it up, and of course out jumped the three nifty little men, and they spoke to him just as if he were Jack, asking him what he wanted.

"You can get rid of this overrated castle for a start," the servant growled. "Take it over the seas and far away, as quick as you can."

Before he'd finished the sentence, the castle started to rise up in the air, pillars and all, and in his fright the servant dropped the snuffbox and jumped off the drawbridge—too late!—and was dashed to pieces on the rocks below. So that was the end of him.

But can you just imagine how annoyed the lord was, and how horrified Jack was, and how his new wife burst into tears, and how everyone set up a huge fuss and pandemonium when they came home from their dancing and found that the wonderful golden castle had disappeared from sight, just as if it had never been?

"You're a cheat and a liar," the lord bellowed to Jack. "You deserve to be beheaded."

But his daughter burst into tears all over again and begged her father to spare Jack's life, and her father relented. "Well, I won't behead you," he said.

"But you must get out of my sight," he roared. "You are banished from my land. I'll give you one year to find the castle and bring it right back here, or you'll never see my daughter again."

✤ *Thump. Thump. Thump.*

A noise was coming from down below. Jack jumped and stopped at once. Jill and the cat stared at the door, and they were ice cold with fright. Someone was coming up the stairs. *Stamp stamp STAMP.* Jack felt for Jill's hand and squeezed it. The someone stood just outside the doorway.

"Fee, fie, fo, fum!" a deep voice bellowed. "I am the giant Cormoran!"

Jill jumped to her feet. "Hide the belt, hide the belt, quickly!" she whispered.

Jack tried to pick up the belt, but his hands were trembling so much that the buckle clattered along the floorboards.

"Fee, fie, fo, fum!" the voice bellowed again. "I hear the bones of an Englishman!"

"No!" squeaked Jack.

"Fee, fie, fo, fum, I smell the blood of an Englishman!"

"No," squeaked Jack again. "I'm not a man. Not yet. I'm only a boy really."

"Fee, fie, fo, fum, here's grub
    for the giant Cormoran!
Bring me Jack, and bring me Jill,
And bring me the cat,
    so I can eat my fill."

At that the cat leaped onto Jill's shoulder, trembling in every bone of his body.

"I'm not scared of you!" he shrieked, his eyes tight closed. "Don't come any nearer, you wicked old giant, or I'll rip you to pieces with my claws!"

The door was flung open, and in came a raggedy man in a tattered brown cloak.

"You're not a giant!" said the cat, collapsing into a furry black heap with relief. "You're not even very tall!"

The man threw back his hood and laughed. "And the giant Cormoran was killed many years ago. Surely you knew that, young Jack."

"You're the man who gave me this bag!" Jill said.

"And you're the man who gave me the beans in exchange for our cow, Blossom!" Jack said.

The man laughed again. He came up to them and clasped their hands warmly in both his own. "And I gave you both a bit of a fright just then, did I? Sorry about that. But I came upstairs before, and you didn't even hear me. You looked so cozy, the three of you, curled up by the fire like that, all wrapped up in the story! I hadn't the heart to interrupt you. The only way I could break the spell was by starting an even better story and pretending to be a giant."

"I wasn't scared," bragged the cat, strutting up to him. "I'm brave these days."

"So I've noticed. I hoped you would be. And Jack has found the belt, and Jill has found Jack, so everything's coming on very nicely, just as I wanted. Oh, how I could do with a bit of that bread and cheese." He sat down heavily on the floor. "Don't mind me. I'm only the Old Feller Storyteller. Been traveling around for donkey's years, head full of stories and feet full of blisters, and I always get paid with bread and cheese."

He began to eat noisily, chuckling to himself from time to time.

"Rip me up, would you?" he said to the cat. The cat gave him a green, unblinking glare. When the old man had finished eating, he dusted the breadcrumbs off his tangled beard and said, "Now, before I forget, you've got to get home quick, Jack. Your mother needs you at once."

"Does she?" said Jack, pleased. "But I'd rather wait till it's light. If I swim in the wrong direction, I might end up in another country!"

"Oh, don't bother swimming! How would he go in a story, Jill? Like this?"

And before she could speak, Old Feller Storyteller fanned out his fingers and blew through them three times, so his breath rippled like little waves, and Jack just disappeared. The cat sniffed the floor where he'd been standing, puzzled.

"Very good!" said Jill. "But I wish I knew what was going on. Can I go with him?"

"Oh, not yet," the old man said. "You're halfway through a story, aren't you? Don't you want to hear the end of it?"

"And another jenny wren came . . ." the cat began helpfully.

But Old Feller Storyteller picked up the snuffbox and rubbed it till it came up gleaming again and, without taking his eyes off Jill, slowly lifted the lid. Out came the sound of a young woman crying and people shouting. He closed it and opened it up again, and there came the sound of a rushing wind that filled up the room and died away to a whisper.

Now, the wonderful castle had gone, and Great-grand-uncle Jack had been banished from the land until he found it and brought it back again. So he said a tearful good-bye to his wife and set off on a journey around the world to find the golden castle, though he had no idea in his heart or his head where he might look for it. He walked and walked, and he knew he should never have asked his mother for that big cake after all. A cake is soon eaten, however big it is. But who knows how long a curse will last?

One day when he was overcome with tiredness and misery, Jack sat down under a willow tree and shared the last few crumbs from his pocket with a mouse, and told him his story, and asked him if he'd seen a golden castle anywhere. The mouse nibbled and thought and shivered his whiskers and then took him to see his mouse king, and he sent a message to all the mice in the world. But word came back by next morning that none of them had seen the golden castle on its twelve mighty pillars.

"Then everything's lost, and I'll never see my wife again!" Jack sighed.

"Oh, don't give up yet! Maybe the frogs could help you," the mouse said, and he tucked himself inside Jack's pocket and led him over the rocks and through the woods and down to the boggy places where frogs like to live. They told Jack's story to a little green frog.

"Have you ever seen a castle like that?" the mouse asked, and the frog bubbled and gulped and bulged out his eyes and then disappeared under the slimy water to tell the king of the frogs. So a message was sent to all the frogs in the world, but next morning word came back that not one of them had seen a golden castle like the one Jack described.

"I'll never see my wife again," Jack said, and tears like rivers ran down his cheeks. "All our children were going to be as clever as I am, but I'm not clever at all!"

"Now stop that," said the frog. "We've still got the birds to ask, and they fly over seas and mountains and all the places that we've never even seen. They'll help, if anyone can." And he hopped into Jack's other pocket, and they went on their way. At last they came to the craggy place where the king of all the birds lived, and they told their story.

"Have you ever come across a castle like that?" the frog asked.

The king of the birds cocked his head this way and that way, and ruffled out his feathers, and whistled deep in his throat, and thought for a long time. He called together all the birds of the air, of the trees and forests and the meadows, of the mountains and the seas, and asked them if any of them had seen a mighty castle standing on twelve golden pillars. But none of them had.

"That's it then," said Jack, sad to his very bones. "Thank you for all your help, my friends. Now I know it's all over, and I'll never see my wife again, and we'll never have children as beautiful as she is, like I promised her."

He slowly turned and began to walk away.

"Wait a minute," called the king of the birds. "One of us is missing. Has anyone seen the eagle?"

Just as he spoke, there came a distant shrill, yelping cry, and high up in the sky, and far away, they could just make out the shape of a soaring eagle. Down it drifted toward them, with its huge wings glinting under the sun, and as it flew, it cried out that it had just come from that very castle that they were searching for and that if Jack had the heart to go with him, he would take him there.

"Indeed I have," said Jack. His blood sang with joy, and the mouse squeaked cheerfully and jumped into one of his pockets, and the frog bubbled happily and jumped into the other, and Jack climbed onto the eagle's back. Off they flew into the cold wind of the starry night, and when dawn came, they reached the castle, perched on the summit of a mountain that was blue with snow.

The eagle set Jack down in front of the great studded door. But the door was locked and barred, and nothing would budge it.

"Well, I've found my castle," said Jack. "But how can I get into it, and how can I get it home? I need the snuffbox, and I've no idea where to find that."

"Let me look," said the mouse, and he crawled out of Jack's pocket and under the great door of the castle and was gone for ages. It was dark by the time he scurried out, but he had the snuffbox in his paws, and he scrambled back into Jack's pocket with it.

Jack looked at the moon and saw that it was almost completely round, and he knew that soon it would be huge and full for the twelfth time. "Quick, we must get away. The year is nearly up!" he said. "I must see my wife again."

Away they soared on the eagle's back. But Jack was so anxious to see the snuffbox that he took it out of his pocket. He held it up so he could admire the way it gleamed in the moonlight, but oh! it slipped out of his fingers and plunged down into the sea.

"Now what have I done?" he sobbed, and now he was no longer full of pride and joy, but beside himself with misery. "I'll never see my wife again, never, and it's all my fault."

"Now stop that!" said the frog. "It's my turn to help you now." He jumped out of Jack's pocket and dived down into the sea. He was missing all night, and the moon faded and the sun rose before he swam up to the surface with the snuffbox in his mouth. Jack leaned down from the eagle's back and scooped them both up, frog and snuffbox, and put them safe and sound in his pocket.

The eagle flew through the day and through the next night, he flew over white mountains and purple seas, he flew over blue forests and meadows yellow with flowers, all the way to the mansion where Jack's young wife and her father lived. There he dropped Jack gently onto the grassy clearing.

"Good-bye, mighty eagle!" Jack called as the great bird soared back up into the clouds. "Thank you for helping me." He could see lights in the mansion, and he knew that day was beginning there, but he daren't show himself yet.

He said good-bye to the frog and the mouse who had done such wonderful things to help him, and then he was all on his own again, looking at the mound where the mighty castle used to be. Was it possible to bring it back? He drew the snuffbox out of his pocket and slowly opened it up, and quick as a flash, out jumped the three little men, bowing and nodding and as eager to help as ever.

"I have only one more thing to ask you," Jack said. "Could you bring me the castle and put it just where it was before, as if it had never been away?"

"Close your eyes," they told him, and Jack did, and behind his eyes he saw a hazy, swirling golden mist, and inside his head he heard a rushing, tempestuous wind such as he'd never heard before. When it died away, he heard such a shouting and cheering that he just had to open his eyes again. There was the castle with its twelve golden pillars, back on its mound overlooking the mansion, and as proud and mighty as any castle you could dream of. And there were the hundred soldiers marching up and down its courtyard, and there were the servants opening the doors and letting in the day.

And up from the mansion came the lord with his arms opened wide to welcome Jack home, and behind him, as full of smiles as ever, came Jack's wife. What did she have in her arms but a beautiful baby.

Jack and his wife forgave the lord because they were so happy to be with each other again. They made the castle their home, and they filled it with children. Ah, and of course, they were happy for the rest of their days.

✤ The Old Feller Storyteller bent down and touched Jill's cheek. She and the cat were curled up together on the hearth, nearly drifting into dreams, in the way that stories take you. "Open your eyes, Jill," the old man said. And when she did, there she was in Old Mother Greenwood's house, and it was day.

The first thing Jill noticed was that the belt was back on its hook by the fire.

The second thing was that even though sunlight and birdsong were pouring through the open door, there was hardly any daylight at all coming through the window. It seemed to be covered with something that gave off a rustling, dull green glow. She ran outside and gazed up at a huge beanstalk that towered over the roof of the house. Mother Greenwood was picking pods of beans off the lower branches and putting them in the pocket of her apron.

"Jack tells me you met the Old Feller," she said to Jill.

"He told me a lovely story." Jill rubbed her eyes and yawned, still wondering whether she was asleep or awake or whether it was night or day, and whether she really was in Mother

Greenwood's garden or still in the giant's castle listening to a story. "It's the best I've ever heard."

"Him and his stories!" Mother Greenwood shook her head and tutted behind her teeth. "I don't know. Sometimes they're worth hearing, and sometimes they bring a load of trouble. Like this thing, for instance. Fancy making it happen in my backyard."

"It's got a lot of beans on it," said Jill.

"If that was all it had, we'd be all right," said the old woman. "But I don't trust him to leave it at that. That's why I sent for Jack. He climbed up it this morning." She peered anxiously up into the swaying branches. "But whether he'll ever come down again is another matter."

They went back into the house and sat at the table together, slicing up the beans to put in the cooking pot.

"And another thing about that Old Feller," said Mother Greenwood. "Everyone he meets has to be put into a story. Like you."

"Like me!" Jill laughed. "I'm not in a story!"

"Oh, yes, you are." Mother Greenwood picked up the pot and put it on its hook over the fire. Then she tipped the cat out of her chair and sat down. Jill came and sat at her feet on the patchy hearthrug, stroking the cat. She had a strange feeling that people were coming into the room behind her, but when she turned around, there was no one to be seen. She looked back into the leaping flames of the fire, and she could sense rather than hear the tiptoe of feet, the rustle and swish of clothes, the creak of chairs, the sighs and whispers of people settling down and making themselves comfortable.

"It's all right," Mother Greenwood said, and her voice was softer than the flurrying sound the fire made. "They've come to hear the last story, that's all."

Jill looked at the belt and knew that at last she was going to hear its story and that she was ready for it. The cat lifted up his head, wise and patient and quiet, and she knew that he was ready, too.

"Lift it down," Mother Greenwood said, and Jill put out her hand. But as soon as her fingers touched the buckle, darkness closed around them, as if the sun had turned black in the sky outside. A wind like a mighty voice howled around the trees of the forest. The great beanstalk swayed and crashed against the side of the cottage, pounding against the window like beating hands. And the letters on the belt gleamed like many tiny eyes: *Hem yu an Kernow harth ha yonk neb a lathas an cawr Cormoran.*

"Read it, Jill." And as Jill spoke the words, they took the sounds of English, and she understood every one of them: "This is the brave young Cornishman who slew the giant Cormoran."

The cat buried his head into Jill's lap, but he stayed where he was.

"Ah, yes, you're ready now." Mother Greenwood's voice came hushing into the darkness. "This belt belonged to young Jack's grandfather. My father. And he was the bravest man who ever lived. He was Jack the Giant Killer. And this is his story."

JACK THE GIANT KILLER

A long time ago, when there were giants who ate people up, the wickedest giant of all was Galligantus. He had a clever conjurer who helped him by tricks and magic to lure knights and ladies into his castle, and as soon as they were there, he would turn them into pigs and weasels, knobbly oak trees, slimy stones, anything that took his fancy.

One day he and his conjurer were traveling through the sky in a burning chariot drawn by fiery dragons. Far below them they saw a beautiful young girl in a duke's garden.

"I'll have her!" Galligantus laughed with a great roar that made all the birds dive away in fright. Down plunged the chariot, and Galligantus leaned out and snatched the girl up, while her white-haired father wept with grief and rage.

Galligantus set her down in the grounds of his castle, and his conjurer turned her into a white deer. Brave young lords and knights from here, there, and everywhere tried to rescue her, but they met with their doom, every one. At the gates of the castle were two fierce griffins with boiling orange eyes and nasty claws, and if anyone came near them, they ripped them to shreds, and then the giant gobbled them up. It was said that the country would never be rid of giants until Galligantus was killed.

Now, far away from Galligantus's castle, in Cornwall, there lived a woodcutter who had a son called Jack. They had a giant of their own in those parts, and he was called Cormoran. He was three times the height of the tallest man in Cornwall, and three times as fat. He lived on an island called St. Michael's Mount, and whenever he was hungry, he would just wade across to the mainland and snatch up anything in sight, cows or pigs or oxen, horses even; he would just tie them around his waist and take them home and gobble them up.

Well, the people of Cornwall had had

enough of him. One night young Jack, who was very brave, decided to do something about it. He took a horn, a shovel, and a pickax over to the island, and with his shovel he dug a deep hole as big as a house, and he covered it over with branches and leaves. Then he put his horn to his lips and blew a loud tantivy, which woke up the giant at once. Out he rushed, full of headache and bad temper.

"What do you mean by waking me up with that row?" he shouted in his bellowy voice. "Come here and be caught, and I'll boil you up with my porridge." But Jack had no intention of being caught or boiled, and as he ran away, the giant blundered after him and tumbled into the hole Jack had dug. Jack struck him dead with the pickax and buried him, and that was the end of the giant Cormoran.

The celebrating went on for days. The mayor presented Jack with a sword and gave him a belt engraved with these words: *Hem yu an Kernow harth ha yonk neb a lathas an cawr Cormoran.*

From now on, he said, Jack would be known as Jack the Giant Killer.

Now, about a hundred miles away there was another giant called Blunderboar. One day when he was out looking for food, he came across Jack, who was fast asleep by a waterfall. He looked at Jack's belt and read the words that were engraved on it and nodded with great satisfaction.

"So you're Jack the Giant Killer, who killed my little brother Cormoran!" he muttered. "I've been wanting to meet you for ages." And he picked Jack up and slung him over his shoulder like a dead rabbit and strode off with him to his enchanted castle.

Jack knew nothing at all about it until they were scrunching through the thicket around the castle. He was very surprised when he realized that he was hanging upside down over the back of a giant.

But there was worse to come.

Blunderboar strode on into a courtyard that was littered with the bones and skulls of all the men he had ever caught. "Yours will be there soon." He chuckled, licking his lips. He dropped Jack inside a blue chamber and locked the door. "Wait there. I'm just going to invite a friend to supper." And off he strode.

All around him Jack could hear the screams and groans of the dead, and they were crying out to him:

"Run! Hide! Get away!
They'll eat you up this very day!"

On and on the voices kept crying out, and Jack didn't know what to do with himself for fright. He looked out of the window, and he saw the two giants coming across the hills together.

"Run! Hide! Get away!
They'll eat you up this very day!"

There were some ropes in the room, and quickly Jack tied them together to make a noose. He could hear the giants' feet going *thud, thud, thud* right up to the iron gate of the castle. He could hear them rattling the keys.

"Run! Hide! Get away!
They'll eat you up this very day!"

Jack leaned out of the window and flung out the rope, swinging it till the noose looped over both the giants' heads at once. He pulled the other end of the rope over a beam and hauled on it

with all his strength and tied it there.
Then he slid down the rope, shouting,

> "Know me now, know my fame,
> Jack the Giant Killer is my
> name!"

and he killed the giants with his sword.
He chopped off their heads and sent
them to the king, and that was the end
of Blunderboar and his friend.

Inside the castle Jack found out that
it was not the dead who had been
screaming out to him, but three young
women who were tied by their long
hair to the ceiling, starving to death
and begging for mercy. Jack helped
them down and gave them the keys
of the castle so they could help
themselves to Blunderboar's treasure.
And he set off for the country of
Wales.

Well, before long he was tired and

hungry and had lost his way, and he knocked on the gates of a castle to ask if he could spend the night there. He was a little put out when the gate was opened by a giant with two heads, but as he was a Welsh giant, he didn't seem quite so much of a monster as the others had been. He was a very friendly giant. He welcomed Jack as if he were his long-lost friend, gave him wine and fruitcake, and offered him a bed for the night.

Jack was singing a little song to himself as he was getting undressed that night and was surprised to hear the giant singing in the room next door, in a very melodious voice. Jack liked the tune, he liked the voice, but he didn't like the words at all:

"Make yourself at home,
    my friend,

But soon your merry ways
    will end.
Before you get up from your bed,
My cudgel will have bashed
    your head."

"Aha," said Jack, "he's just like all the other giants after all. I might have known." So he put a bolster in his bed and hid behind the door, and during the night the giant crept in with his cudgel and swung it across the bolster many times till he was quite sure he had finished Jack off. Next morning he was amazed when Jack came down to breakfast.

"Didn't you feel something during the night?" he asked Jack, and Jack just looked surprised and said, "Nothing much, only a little mouse scampering over me in my bed. It tickled a bit." But he hadn't finished with the giant yet.

Oh, no. "Can I have some breakfast?" he asked. "It smells delicious." And the giant was so surprised that he gave Jack a huge bowl of rice pudding that would have fed ten men and left some over for supper.

When the giant wasn't looking, Jack slid the pudding into a bag and hid it under his shirt, and then he said to the giant, "Do you want to see a trick?"

He took a knife and slit open the bag, as if he were slitting open his belly, and out slopped the pudding. "I bet you can't do that."

"Simple pimple!" said the giant. He snatched the knife from Jack and slit his own belly in half. Out fell all his blubbery bits, flopperty all over the floor, and he dropped down dead. Jack chopped off his heads and sent them to the king, and that was the end of the Welsh giant.

Well, Jack went on his way, and it wasn't long before he needed somewhere to sleep. He remembered then that he had a very distant and very huge cousin who lived just two miles away. This cousin happened to have three heads, and could fight five hundred men in armor, and had a lot of giant ways about him. But he was Jack's cousin all the same.

Jack hammered on the castle gate. "Wake up!" he shouted. "It's your cousin Jack, and I've come to warn you that the king is approaching with a huge army."

"Pooh, what do I care? Pooh, what do I care? Pooh, what do I care?" The cousin with three heads laughed. "I can fight five hundred soldiers in armor and blow them away like dandelion seeds. Dandelion seeds. Lion seeds."

"But the king has a thousand

soldiers," Jack told him. "A thousand!"

I forgot to say that this very distant cousin was also a coward, and he ran and hid in the vault and stayed there trembling like a mouse all night while Jack feasted on his food and slept in his great comfortable bed. Next morning Jack called down to his cousin that it was safe for him to come out of the vault.

"Thank you for protecting my castle," the cousin said, brushing cobwebs and spiders out of his three beards. "What can I give you to show my gratitude? Gratitude? Attitude?"

"I've seen a cap and a coat, a sword, and shoes by your bed," said Jack. "Can I take those?"

"Take them with all my heart, all my heart, my heart, with all of them," said the cousin. "The coat will keep you invisible, the cap will give you knowledge, the shoes will bring you swiftness, and the sword will cut in half whatever it strikes. Take them, they're yours. They're yours. Yours." And the three-headed, very distant cousin closed his castle gates and never did anything to frighten anyone smaller than himself again.

So Jack went on his way. He rode for three days over the high, green, wet mountains of Wales and only stopped when he heard such pitiful cries that he knew someone was in danger and that he had to help. He saw a terrible sight. A huge red-haired monster of a giant was dangling a knight and a lady by the hair, taunting them and tickling them and teasing them and smacking his lips because he was so near to gobbling them up.

Jack put on his coat of invisibility and ran right up to the giant, swinging his wonderful sword backward and forward. He managed to send him crashing down with such a smash that the whole ground shook for five miles around. Then he put his foot on the giant's neck and said, "Take this for your villainy, and say good-bye to your head." He chopped off his head and sent it to the king, and that was the end of the red-headed giant.

The knight and lady thanked Jack for saving their lives and begged him to come back with them to their castle, but he refused. "I must find this giant's den and set free all his prisoners," he said.

"Don't go there," they warned him. "He has a brother who is even worse than he is. Please don't risk your life again."

"I am Jack the Giant Killer," he said.

"I don't care how many giants there are. I shan't rest until I've slain them all."

And sure enough, before that day was out, he had found the den of the giants. The brother was sitting outside his cave with his cudgel at his side. Jack had never seen a more hideous giant. His eyes were like cauldrons of bubbling green oil, and his hair was like wriggling snakes. His cheeks were as red and thick as sides of raw bacon, and his hairy hands were bigger than barrels. Oh, and he smelled like a bin of rotten eggs.

Jack put on his coat of invisibility and crept up to him and whispered, "I am Jack the Giant Killer, and I've come to chop off your head."

The giant looked this way and that, but there was nothing to see.

"I am Jack the Giant Killer. Say

good-bye to your head," Jack whispered again, and again the giant looked this way and that and shrugged his shoulders, which were like wardrobe doors.

Then Jack charged at him with his wonderful sword and missed the neck but cut off the nose, which bounced down the hill and set the giant roaring after it like a bull. Jack charged again and stuck the sword in fast, and the giant tottered around for about an hour and then dropped down to the ground with a mighty, thundering crash. Jack cut off his head and sent it to the king, and that was the end of the ugliest giant in the world.

Then Jack ran into the den and set all the giants' prisoners free. They all danced down to the village, cheering and singing as they went, "The giants are dead, the giants are dead!" They lifted Jack onto their shoulders and cheered till their throats were dry. But a child from the village came running up with his eyes nearly bursting out of his head.

"Thunderdell is coming!" he shouted. "Take shelter, hide!"

Now two-headed Thunderdell was the fiercest giant in the whole of North Wales. As he strode toward them, the ground began to heave and shake as if the world were breaking in half; trees crashed to the ground, and hills collapsed into heaps of dust.

"Who killed my brothers?" he roared. "Let me grind up his bones. Let me guzzle his blood!"

Everybody fled, screaming. Everybody, that is, except Jack.

"Let him come," he said calmly. "I am Jack the Giant Killer. I will pick his teeth with my sword."

Now, Jack had a clever plan in his head. The village castle was surrounded by a moat that was full of deep, freezing water. Jack asked the men to cut the bridge into three parts, so the middle part would sink when any weight was put upon it. They had just finished when the giant strode over the last hill and stood glaring down at the village. The men rushed for shelter. But Jack put on his coat of invisibility and his shoes of swiftness. He took up his wonderful sword, and he danced up to the giant Thunderdell.

Well, even though the giant couldn't see Jack, he could smell him with both his noses. *Sniff sniff!* he went. *Sniff sniff.*

"Fee, fie, foe, fum, I smell the blood of a Cornishman!" he bellowed, and the mountains rang and shivered with the sound of his voice.

"Fee, fie, foe, fum,
I smell the blood of
    an Englishman.
Be he alive or be he dead,
I'll grind his bones
    to make my bread!"

"Oh, will you indeed?" shouted Jack, and he threw off his coat of invisibility and stood, tiny and brave, at the giant's feet.

Thunderdell snatched out for him, and Jack dodged away. Thunderdell snatched again, and Jack dodged away. Thunderdell snatched again, and Jack ran as if he were afraid for his life, and his shoes of swiftness took him as fast as a hare and as light as a bird over the bridge and into the castle. The giant blundered after him, but he was so heavy that the middle part of the bridge sank down into the moat, and he sank with it. He wallowed in the water like a great blubbery whale, bellowing his head off.

"A fine bully you are!" shouted Jack. "A fine monster! Frightened of having a cold bath, are you?" He threw a noose around the giant's two heads, and with a team of strong jet black horses he dragged him out of the water. Then he chopped off both his heads and sent them to the king, and that was the end of Thunderdell.

The rejoicing in the castle lasted for days, but Jack wasn't finished yet. Oh, no. He journeyed on his way, and one night he met an old man with snow white hair.

"Are you Jack the Giant Killer?" the old man asked him.

"I am," said Jack. "And I will not rest until all the giants are slain."

"Well, there's one left," said the old man. "And he is the cleverest of all, because he has a conjurer to help him."

And he told Jack the story of Galligantus, and his conjurer, and his fierce griffins and his burning chariot, and the people in the enchanted castle who had been turned into pigs and weasels and knobbly oak trees and slimy stones, and his own beautiful daughter, who was a white deer.

"Many men have tried to rescue her," he said sadly. "And they've perished, every one."

"Then let me try," said Jack.

"If you will. Let cunning defeat cunning, and magic defeat magic," the old man said. "There's no other way." He put his arms around Jack and embraced him, and there were tears of hope in his eyes. "Go wisely and safely.

Look for a golden song on a silver thread."

Jack put on his coat of invisibility and his shoes of swiftness and his cap of knowledge, and picked up his wonderful sword, and he knew that his greatest victory was still to come.

It was the dawn of the day when he climbed the mountain up to the enchanted castle. He saw the fierce griffins with their boiling orange eyes and nasty claws, and they snatched out into the empty air at him, snarling and spitting, but he passed between them unseen into the courtyard. He saw all around him knobbly trees and slimy stones, weasels and stoats, toads and lizards, a beautiful white deer, and they all had the eyes of humans, and all the eyes were fixed upon him, begging him soundlessly to break the curse and set them free.

He searched the grounds, and at last looked down a deep well and found what he was looking for. Hanging inside the well was a golden trumpet on a silver chain. He lifted it out, and this is what was written on it:

Blow this trumpet loud and shrill.
You will Galligantus kill.
Break the magic of his spell,
And all the country shall be well.

And Jack the Giant Killer lifted the trumpet to his lips and blew on it. In their tower Galligantus and his conjurer clung to each other, shivering with fear, because they knew that someone stronger and braver and cleverer than they were had entered the castle. It

must be another giant, huger than
any Galligantus, they thought. Or a
magician who had lived a thousand
years, if he knew more magic than the
conjurer did. The trumpet sounded
again. They peered over the parapet,
and there was no one to be seen.
A third time the trumpet sounded.

Then they heard a whispery, dancy
voice that came from nowhere, that
sang in the air around their heads—
"Know me now, know my fame, Jack
the Giant Killer is my name"—and that
tiny voice struck terror into their
hearts.

Galligantus stooped down on his
hands and knees to pick up his cudgel,
and in an instant Jack swiped off his
head with a single blow of his sword.
The conjurer shrieked for mercy and
rose into the air and was sucked up

into the very heart of a spinning whirlwind, never, ever to be seen again.

The spell was broken. The pigs and stoats, the oak trees and stones, and all the other strange shapes became people again, full of wonder and joy at their release. The white deer turned into a beautiful young girl. Jack fell in love with her and asked her if she would marry him. And the beautiful young girl said, "Yes."

The whole country celebrated because the giants had gone forever. And Jack the Giant Killer and his lady lived in peace and happiness for the rest of their days.

✤ "Ah!" sighed Jill, and realized that she had been holding her breath for a long time. "That's the best story I've ever heard in my life."

The darkness around her began to lift away like smoke, and in the room she could see dim shapes now, stirring and stretching—an old man with a long beard, a young man tanned from the fields, a rich man in velvets, and a poor man in rags—and Jill knew that they were all the Jacks of the stories, listening again to the tales of their fame. But as the sun poured at last through the doorway, the shapes had gone, and she was left alone with the old woman and the purring cat.

"Did you see all the Jacks?" Mother Greenwood said. "How they do love to hear their stories told! Famous, they are!"

"I didn't see my Jack," said Jill. "I mean, your Jack," she added quickly. "Your son."

"Ah, now I've got a feeling in my bones that he's going to be the most famous Jack of all, if he does things right," the old woman said. "But just at this moment he's stuck up that darned beanstalk, and he doesn't know what to do next."

"Can I do anything to help him?" Jill asked.

"What do you think, Cat? Shall we let her?"

The cat yawned and licked himself and stretched and curled up tight and tidy again.

"He doesn't know," said Mother Greenwood. "After all, he's only a cat!"

She lifted up the belt and stroked it lovingly. Then she led Jill outside and gazed up at the swaying beanstalk.

"I would like Jack to have this belt," she said. "In memory of his grandfather. Then I think he'll know what to do. Will you take it to him?"

Jill hesitated for a moment. She thought about all the Jacks she had come to know since she met Mother Greenwood. She remembered the fishbone comb and the rusty needle and the little grain of corn. She remembered the golden ball that had turned into an apple, and she remembered the snuffbox. And then she thought about the pouch of beans. Was there a story about that, too? she wondered. And would Jack be famous one day because of it? She took the belt and fastened it around her waist for safety. And then she put one hand on the first branch, and one hand on the second, and climbed up and up into the swirling green of the beanstalk, and was soon out of sight.

An old man in a tattered cloak passed by the gate and waved to Mother Greenwood.

"Come in, Old Feller!" she called to him, and he followed her into the cottage. She cut up some bread and cheese for him, and they sat each side of the fire, looking at the whispering flames and hearing secrets in them.

"Maybe my father didn't kill all the giants, after all," she said. Old Feller Storyteller raised his eyebrows and stroked his beard and said nothing for a while.

"There's one giant left," he told her at last.

"Ah," purred the cat in his deep sleep. "But that's another story."

BERLIE DOHERTY is the author of numerous books for children and young adults. She has won the prestigious Carnegie Medal twice—for *Granny Was a Buffer Girl* and for *Dear Nobody*—and in 1994 *Willa and Old Miss Annie* was highly commended for the Carnegie Medal. Ms. Doherty began writing tales even before she went to school and at age eight was earning boxes of chocolates and boxes of paints from the local newspapers for her stories and poems. She lives in England.